Illustrations by Cameron Wilson for Soulsimplicity Design and Publishing.

This book is dedicated to my children Maya and Samuel Fenderson. Also I dedicate this to my nieces, cousins and to all that dear to dream larger than your circumstances. Ajani, Jalia, Ashai, Amaan, Asahn, Aison, Uriella, Quinn, Lily, Aliah, Daryll, Johanna, Vance, Zulekha, Jomo, Jamal, Mark, Mikael, Samira, Ameerah, Sahar, Nasir, Arriana, Breanna, Jayden, Reagan, Ryan, Madison, Noah,Tony, Czarina

Moni's DREAMS COME TRUE!

BY MONICA FENDERSON
ILLUSTRATED BY
CAMERON WILSON
EDITED BY VICKI BINGHAM

Moni is a little girl from Brooklyn, New York living with her mom and four other siblings. Her neighborhood was rough. It was full of crime, pollution and abandon buildings. Moni uses her imagination to change her environment.

Moni went to sleep and had a dream. She saw her drawings coming to life. She was on a construction site in her neighborhood. Moni was designing beautiful buildings and parks.

Moni's brother took her to a Bodega, a small store with beautiful colors on the outside. She started daydreaming while eating the ice cream. The world is full of all types of shapes, textures and colors.

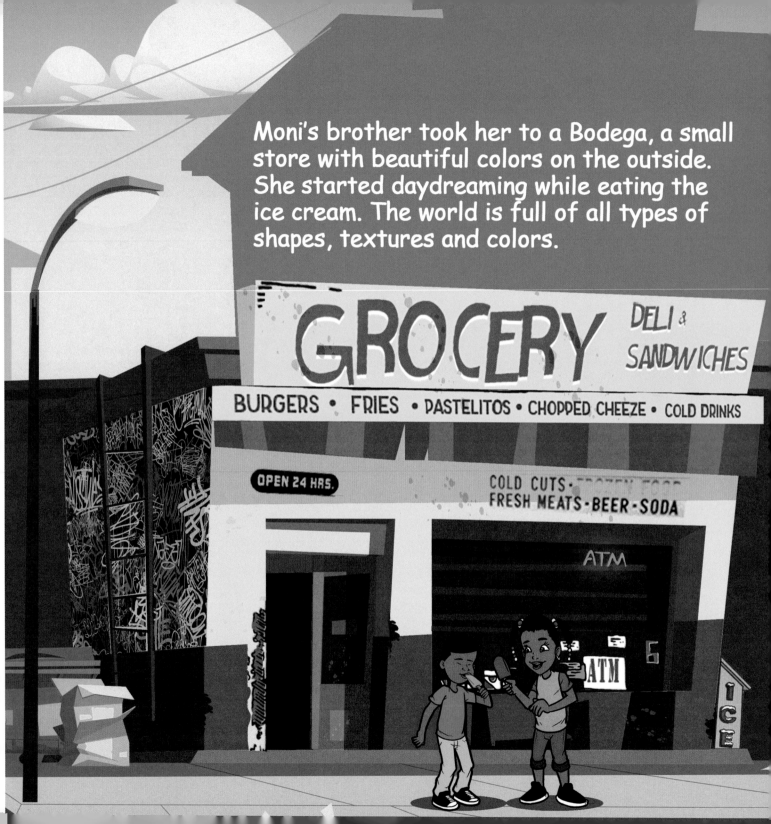

Moni was lucky to have brothers and sisters to show her around New York City; Coney Island, Brooklyn Bridge, The Bronx Zoo, and the beautiful skyscrapers.

Moni had a dream about the beautiful parks and buildings she had seen in New York. She says to herself, "One day I will build lots of beautiful buildings in my neighborhood."

Moni asks her brother "Why do some neighborhoods look better than others?" She sees that some areas had spotless streets, colorful flowers and trees, and unique buildings with special designs.

Moni had a babysitter from Haiti, that would take her to a beautiful park to play. She encouraged Moni to dream big. The park had basketball hoops, hopscotch, swings, and a slide. The park seemed safer and prettier than the one in her neighborhood. She really wished she had a nice park in her community.

Moni was so excited about her plans that she had put together for her future. She jumped around and danced with joy. She figured out what she wanted to be when she grew up. Moni is going to become a great Architect.

Every day, Moni sat at her desk doodling, sketching, and drawing imaginary neighborhoods. She had learned that an Architect designed buildings. Math and Science was some of Moni's favorite subjects in school. Moni knew she was going to be a great Architect.

At the dinner table, Moni told her family that she had a plan. She was going to be an Architect. Her family did not know what to say, but they knew she had a special gift.

Moni stayed determined to make her dreams come true.

Stepping into the world of becoming a great architect was fun for Moni, because she loved to draw and design cool buildings. Moni had great teachers and internships to help her passion to be an architect.

MOSA|ARCHITECTS

Here are a few things that you need to know to make your dreams come true.

Believe in yourself, write down your dreams, research what it takes to do what you want to become. Always ask questions, respect yourself and others, keep a log of your accomplishments, find a mentor, stay focused, and always have fun!

Words To Remember

Architecture -
The art or practice of designing and constructing buildings.

Architects -
A person who plans designs and oversees the construction of buildings.

Engineers-
An engineer is a person who designs, builds, or maintains engines, machines, or public works.

Technical Drawings-
A precise and detailed drawing of an object, as employed in architecture or engineering.

Civil Engineers-
Deal with the design, construction, and maintenance of the physical and naturally built environment, including public works such as roads, bridges, canals, dams, airports, sewerage systems, pipelines, structural components of buildings, and railways.

Electrical-
Electrical engineering is an engineering discipline concerned with the study, design, and application of equipment, devices, and systems which use electricity, electronics, and electromagnetism.

Mechanical-
A person who designs power producing machines, such as electric generators, internal combustion engines, and steam and gas turbines, as well as power using machines such as refrigeration and air-conditioning systems.

Schematic Design -
In this step, an architect talks with the client to determine the project requirements and goals. Schematic Designers often produces rough drawings of a site plan, floor plans, elevations, and often illustrative sketches or computer renderings.

Facade-
The outside or all of the external faces of a building. The term is frequently used to refer just to the main or front face of a house. An exterior wall, or face, of a building. The front facade of a building contains the building's main entrance, the rear facade is the building's rear exterior wall, and the side facades are a building's side exterior walls.

Floor Plan-
The arrangement of rooms in a building.

About the Author

Monica Fenderson was raised by a single mother who was from Costa Rica, with her 4 older siblings. She lived in "The Junction" of Brooklyn, New York. This area had a high population of mixed cultures from the Caribbean. At the age of seven Monica moved to Long Island, New York. Monica had the opportunity to explore the five boroughs and she discovered a love for neighborhoods, community and design.

As she matured through the years, she decided to become an architect. This profession would be a way for her to reconstruct low-income neighborhoods. In the year 1996 Monica got her bachelor's degree in Architecture at Tuskegee University which is an Historical Black College University (HBCU).

Monica later pursued her aspirations for architecture where she is currently the owner of MOSA Architects.

MONICA FENDERSON

Made in the USA
Middletown, DE
28 April 2023

29662110R00015